The Icky Sticky Chameleon

Written by Dawn Bentley
Illustrated by Jeff Mack

In the Hookalee jungle the animals call home,
There was one little creature who felt all alone.
He felt as blue as the Hookalee sea,
And cried, "I wish there was someone just like me."

Chameleon could change his color at will,
And his long, pink tongue would never stay still.
THWOOP!—out it came, quite by surprise,
It was icky and sticky and twice his size.
He could use it to eat, to play and to swing,
He could use his tongue for most anything!

He had two bulging eyes that looked all around—
While one looked up, the other looked down.
The animals asked him, "What are you looking for?"
"I have lots of friends," he said, "but I want one more.
You all have friends that are exactly like you,
But I'm the only chameleon. I wish there were two."

Giraffe tried to help. "I know what to do—
Climb up my neck for a better view."

THWOOP! Out came his tongue to use like a rope,
And up he climbed to broaden his scope.

But all he saw was a monkey in a tree.
"Hello!" said Monkey. "Come look with me!"

THWOOP! Out came his tongue, and wrapped round the trees—
And he swung through the jungle with the greatest of ease.

They went through the trees as far as they could go,
And came to a river with a friendly hippo.

"I'll help you," said Hippo. "I'll give you a ride.
You might find a chameleon on the other side."

THWOOP! Out came his tongue to use as an oar,
And he and Hippo swam to the shore.

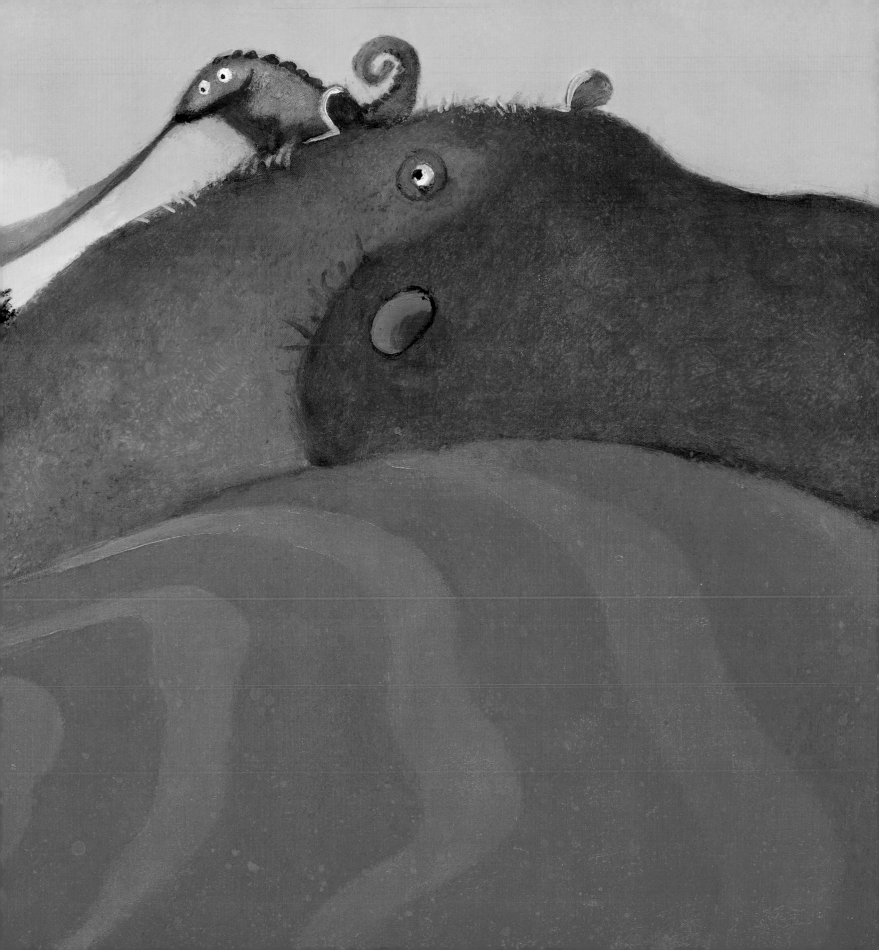

"We'll help you," said Elephant marching in a row.
"Hold onto my tail and off we'll go!"

THWOOP! Out came his tongue and he held on tight.
They searched as they marched—no chameleon in sight!

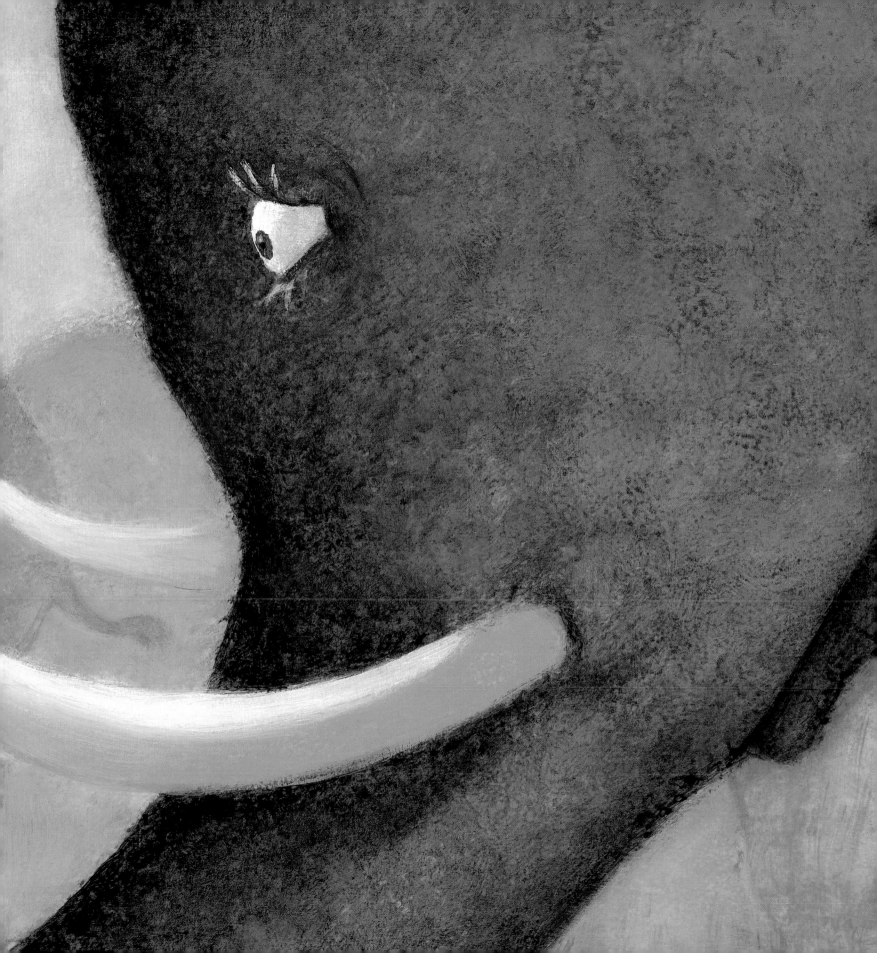

"I'll help!" said Lion, with a mighty roar.
But Chameleon was tired. He could search no more.

THWOOP! Out came his tongue as he climbed back up his tree.
"I guess there aren't any more chameleons in Hookalee."

Then he felt the tickle of a long, sticky tongue.
He looked high and low to see where it came from.

On a branch beside him, behind a leaf so green,
Was the most beautiful chameleon he'd ever seen!

She had amazing wiggly, jiggly eyes.
And a long sticky tongue that was twice her size.
She could change the color of her bumpy skin.
At last he found someone who was just like him!

Chameleon was so happy he could hardly think.
THWOOP! Out came his tongue and he turned tickled pink!